Stories for Four-Year-Olds

by
Margaret Ryan,
Rachel Anderson,
Jean Baylis,
Kate Petty,
Robin Kingsland
and Janie Hampton

Illustrated by Penny Dann

First published in Great Britain by
CollinsChildren'sBooks 1993, a division of
HarperCollins*Publishers* Ltd
77-85 Fulham Palace Road,
Hammersmith, London W6 8JB

3 5 7 9 8 6 4 2

Printed and bound in Great Britain by
Caledonian International Book Manufacturing Limited, Glasgow

Stories for Four-Year-Olds

Other Story Collections in this Series:

Stories for Three-Year-Olds
Stories for Five-Year-Olds
Stories for Six-Year-Olds
Stories for Seven-Year-Olds

CONTENTS

(The times in brackets show approximately how long it takes to read each story aloud.)

CONTENTS

THE LITTLEST DRAGON
by Margaret Ryan

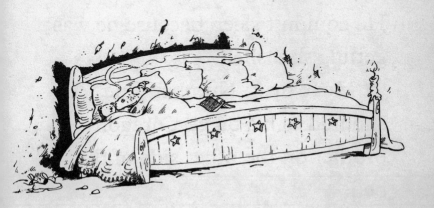

It was deep dark night-time. In the
dragons' cave, ten dragons lay in
the big dragon's bed.

Nine of the dragons were snoring,

but the littlest one, Number Ten, wasn't.

He lay on his side with his nose jammed up against the cave wall. He couldn't sleep because he was getting squashed.

"Move over, Number One," he shouted to his biggest dragon brother on the other side of the bed.

"Snnnnnorrrrre, snnnnorrrrre, snnnorrrrk," said Number One.

"Shove along a bit, Five and Six," he called to his middle-sized brothers who were twins.

"Eeeeee, wheeeee, whistle," said Numbers Five and Six.

"You've got your right elbow in

my ear," he said to Number Nine who was asleep beside him.

"Three blind mice," said Number Nine who always chanted nursery rhymes in his sleep.

"This won't do at all," said the littlest dragon. "I'll never get to sleep at this rate." He wriggled as best he could, and squiggled as best he could. But it was no use, he was sandwiched between the cave wall and his sleeping brothers. Then, he had his first idea.

"Breakfast time, boys," he called in a high voice, very like his mum's.

The big bed shook as nine dragons leapt out of it and headed for the door, shouting, "Oh goody,

I'm starving...", "I want toast soldiers...", "I could eat two basins of porridge...", "Me too...", "Let go of my tail...", "I was first."

The littlest dragon gave a smile and a sigh and snuggled down in the big warm bed. At last he had the bed to himself.

But not for long. Soon the other nine dragons were back.

"It's not breakfast time at all," said Number Eight.

"It's the middle of the night," said Number Four.

"We were sure we heard Mum's voice calling us," said Numbers Five and Six.

"Zzzzzzzzz," said the littlest

dragon. But that soon changed to "Owwwwwww," as all the other dragons piled back into the big bed and squashed his nose back up against the wall.

The littlest dragon rubbed his nose and had a serious think. After a few moments, he had his second idea. He waited till the other dragons were fast asleep and he could count all the different snores.

"Snnnnorrrrre, snnnnorrrre, snnnnorrrrk," went Number One.

"Snnnnnufffffle, snnnnnnuffffle, snniffff," went Number Two.

"Urrk, urrk, oink," went Number Three.

"Burrrrble, burrrrble, boink,"

went Number Four.

"Eeeee, wheeeee, whistle," went Numbers Five and Six.

"Baaaaa, baaaa, baaaaa," went Number Seven who still counted sheep in his sleep.

"Aaaaaarrrrooooooaaaaarrrr," went Number Eight.

"Tom Tom the piper's son," said Number Nine.

"Right," said the littlest dragon and called in a deep voice very like his dad's, "Time for a game of football, boys."

The big bed shook as nine dragons leapt out of it, and headed for the door, shouting, "That's my football jersey, give it back...",

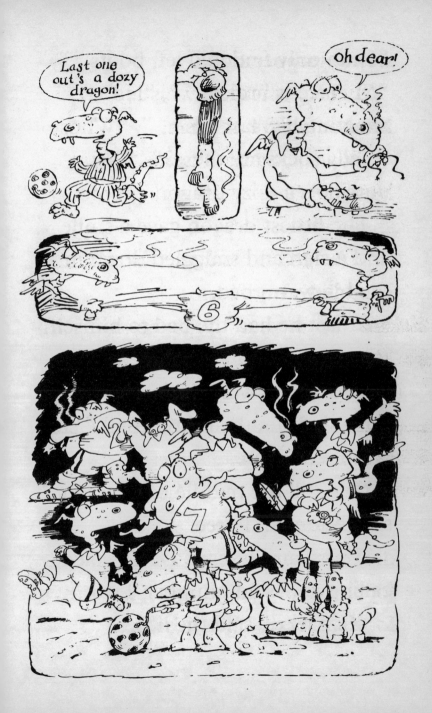

"I can only find two left boots...", "My lace is broken...", "No cheating like last time...", "Whose smelly socks are these?" "Last outside's a dozy dragon...".

The littlest dragon gave a smile and a sigh and snuggled down in the big warm bed.

At last he had the bed to himself. But not for long. Soon the other nine dragons were back.

"It's not football time at all," said Number Seven.

"It's still the middle of the night," said Number Three.

"I was sure I heard Dad's voice calling us," said Number Two.

"Zzzzzzzz," said the littlest

dragon, but that soon changed to "Owwwww," as the dragons piled back into the bed and squashed his nose back up against the wall.

"Thidz idn't bunny," muttered the littlest dragon through his squashed nose.

Then he had his third idea. If he couldn't get to sleep lying beside his brothers, perhaps he could get to sleep lying on top of them.

So he clambered up and lay on brothers Nine, Eight and Seven.

"Get off, Number Ten, and let us get some sleep," they all said and bounced him up into the air.

When he came down, he landed on brothers Six, Five and Four.

"Get off, Number Ten, and don't be such a pest," they all said, and bounced him up even higher into the air.

When he came down, he landed on brothers Three, Two and One.

"Get off, Number Ten. Get back to your own space," they all said and bounced him up so high into the air that he didn't come down again, but landed on a broad ledge near the roof of the cave.

"Oh, dear," said the littlest dragon peering down into the dimly-lit cave, "How am I going to get down from here?" Then he had his fourth and best idea.

"Oh, how nice it is up here," he

said in a squeaky voice. "What a cosy place to sleep. And all to myself too. How nice it is to have a place of my own at last."

"A place of his own?" said the other nine dragons. "We'll soon see about that." And the big bed shook as they all leapt out, got themselves a long ladder and climbed up to join Number Ten.

"It is nice up here," said brothers One, Two and Three, elbowing the littlest dragon out of the way.

"Very cosy," said brothers Four, Five and Six, nudging the littlest dragon over a bit more.

"He can't possibly have it all to himself," said brothers Seven, Eight and Nine. "What about the rest of us?"

"You're quite right," said the littlest dragon hurrying down the long ladder, and pulling it away. "You have it all to yourselves instead."

"Come back with that ladder this minute, Number Ten," shouted the other dragons. "We can't all sleep up here. We'll be squashed."

But the littlest dragon wasn't listening. He'd already climbed back into the big warm dragon's bed, and with a smile and a sigh, snuggled down and went to sleep. "ZZzzzzzzzzzzzz ..."

ASHLEY AND THE POOR FISH
by Rachel Anderson

Ashley's friend lived next door.
Ashley's friend had a dog and a cat,
a budgie and a bike.

Sometimes Ashley wished that he had a pet. Instead, he had a big brother, a big sister and a very old gran.

"And that's quite enough for us to be going on with," said Ashley's mum.

Then, one morning, Ashley's friend from next door came round and swung on the garden gate. Jack from next door had a small fish in a jam jar. It was in a little bit of water and, although it wasn't moving, it was definitely alive.

"Would you like it?" said Jack. "My mum won it but she doesn't want it. Nor do I. It can't do anything. Can't talk, like my

budgie, or do tricks like my dog.
And another thing, my mum says
our cat'll get it if we keep it."

"All right," said Ashley. "I'll look
after it for you."

He carried the jam jar carefully
into the kitchen.

"Look, Mum," he said. "Jack's
given me a fish."

His mother looked into the jam
jar where the fish was trying to
swim but there wasn't much room
for it to turn around.

"What on earth do you want
that for?" said Ashley's mum.
"Poor little thing, it does look
miserable. No, love, don't leave it
on the table. Can't you see I'm

busy baking?"

So Ashley took the jam jar upstairs and showed the fish to his big sister. She was drying her hair.

"Ooeer!" she said. "What horrible eyes it's got. And watch out with that water, Ashley. I don't want it dripping all over my nice new shoes."

So Ashley took the jam jar out to his dad in the shed.

"What's that you've got in there, Ashley?"

"It's a fish," said Ashley. "From Jack."

"Not very big, is it? Hardly worth keeping. Shouldn't think it's got long to live in there either."

Ashley looked at his fish. Was it really so small, so sick-looking and so ugly?

He noticed that Jack's cat had come over from next door. It was sunning itself under the Brussels sprouts stalks and pretending to be asleep. But as Ashley went past with the jam jar, Ashley saw it twitch its tail and blink its eyes.

Ashley hurried back to the kitchen. He took a large glass dish from the cupboard and tipped the fish into it.

"Oh Ashley!" said his mum. "That's my best dish. You know I use that for the fruit salad. I'll be needing it at the weekend, but I suppose you can have it till then."

When it was in the glass dish, the fish looked even smaller than before. It hovered near the bottom hardly moving its fins at all.

"You'll upset that poor creature," said Ashley's sister, "if you keep walking about with it like that."

"It'll probably die of fright anyway," said Ashley's brother turning on the television.

"If Jack's cat doesn't get at it first," added Ashley's sister.

Jack's cat was sitting with its eyes shut on the doorstep of Ashley's house.

"Best thing for it, if you ask me," said Ashley's dad, picking up the evening paper. "I should put it out of its misery if I were you. Make a tasty fishpaste sandwich."

Jack's cat flicked its tail against the front door of Ashley's house.

"What do goldfish eat, Mum?" Ashley asked.

But Mum said, "Don't ask difficult questions just now, love. I'm trying to get the tea."

Apart from Jack's cat, nobody seemed interested in the fish, so Ashley carried the glass dish along to his gran's room.

"Please can I keep my fish in here?" he asked and he put the fish in the dish on her window sill.

Gran didn't say anything. She

had her teeth out, her glasses in her hand and her hearing-aid switched to low. She was having her nap. So Ashley tiptoed quietly out.

At bedtime, when Ashley went to say goodnight to the fish, Gran was awake. She had her teeth in now, her glasses on and her hearing aid switched up. But she couldn't see the fish at all. She was sitting with her back to the window and the curtains were closed. She was busy watching her favourite programme.

"Night Gran," said Ashley. "Night Fish."

Next morning, Ashley's dad said, "So I see you've landed your gran with that poor thing."

Mum said, "Well, I suppose we'd better find it something to eat, hadn't we?"

So when Ashley and Mum were doing the shopping, Mum stopped off at the pet shop and bought a packet of fish food.

"Gravel," said the pet shop assistant. "That's what you could do with. For the bottom of your fish tank." And he gave Ashley a small packet of tiny yellow stones as well.

When Ashley took the fish food to his fish, Gran had her glasses on and was facing towards the fish on the window sill.

"Well now, isn't he a funny little fellow?" she said. "But he's not very well you know, dear."

Ashley helped to pull Gran's chair round the way she liked it with her back to the window. She watched the horses on television while Ashley spread the gravel on the bottom of the glass dish and sprinkled tiny flakes of fish food on the surface of the water. At first, the fish still hovered at the bottom, but then it darted up and grabbed a mouthful of fish flakes.

Gran turned her chair halfway back towards the window so that she could watch both the television and the fish at the same time.

"Well I never!" she said. "Look how he's taking his meal. He's getting quite chirpy."

Later on, Ashley's sister came in to have a look. "He's been swimming all over the place now he's had his tea," said Gran.

"Fancy that," said Ashley's sister. "And he's quite a pretty colour really. Sort of auburn."

When he got in from work, Ashley's dad popped in, too.

"Sprightly little sardine, isn't he?" he said. "Would he like some nice green plants in there? Maybe I'll fetch you some on my way home tomorrow."

Jack's cat came along the passage

to Gran's room, swishing his tail as though he owned the place, but Ashley quickly closed the door before he could get in.

"Now Ashley," said his mum. "Don't forget I'll be needing my fruit salad dish back at the weekend."

"Yes, Mum," said Ashley. He wondered where the fish was going to live. He didn't want to put it back in the jam jar.

Next evening when Ashley's dad came home he had some green water plants in a plastic bag, and he also had a sturdy glass fish tank under his arm.

"Got it off a mate at work," he said.

Ashley put the tank on Gran's window sill. Gran filled it with tepid water from her kettle. Ashley sprinkled some gravel on the bottom of the tank, and Gran and he planted the roots of the water plants in the gravel using one of Gran's knitting-needles. Then they moved the fish to its new home.

Gran sat back in her chair, all worn out.

"It's even more tiring than moving house," she said.

Ashley sat down on the floor beside her and they both watched. At first the fish did nothing. But then it began swimming gracefully between the green leaves of the

water plants, exploring its new home. Then it seemed to get hungry and began searching for fallen fish-flakes in the gravel.

"There we are now," said Gran. "That's better."

When Jack from next door heard how well the fish was doing, he came round to have a look.

"Yes, he's really settled in now," said Ashley.

Jack brought a present for the fish. "It's an underwater ruined castle," he explained. "To put in the tank so that the fish'll have somewhere interesting to visit."

Ashley lowered the ruined castle into the tank, taking care not to frighten the fish or disturb the plants. The fish swam up to the ruined castle, then swam round it, then swam in through the front archway and out through the back.

"Yes," said Ashley. "He likes it."

"Why d'you keep that nice goldfish in Gran's room?" said Ashley's sister. "Why not keep it in the living room? Then we could all enjoy it."

Ashley shook his head. "Jack gave it to me. And I've given it to Gran. It'd be ever so lonely if it didn't have Gran looking after it."

THE JELLY MONSTER
by Jean Baylis

It was a lovely sunny day. The
Browns were having a picnic in the
country. There they were, sitting
round a large spotty table cloth laid

on the grass, happily munching their picnic.

"Mmmm!" said little Anne Brown. "Sandwiches!"

"Yummm!" said little Jim Brown. "Sausage rolls!"

"Delish!" said Daddy Brown, "Lemonade!"

"And now," said Mummy Brown, "JELLY and cream!"

"Yummy!" they all cried, spoons at the ready.

But before anyone had even taken one mouthful, a deep voice said "YUMMY" too. "My favourite! GGGrrrrr!"

Loud, heavy footsteps stomped through the undergrowth and

suddenly a large purple Monster poked his head out of the bushes.

"I love jelly!" said the Monster.

The Browns sat terrified and watched with horror as the Monster crunched his way out of the bushes and gulped all of the jelly in one greedy mouthful. Not one little wobbly bit did he leave.

The Monster burped rudely, rubbed his tummy and rumbled off back into the forest. The Browns were so scared that he would come back and gobble them up too, that they grabbed what was left of their picnic and drove home as quickly as their little car could take them.

Mrs Williams had invited her

nephews over for afternoon tea. There they were, having a lovely time eating all the delicious sandwiches and pies that she had made.

"Now," said Mrs Williams, "I know you love puddings, so I have made a very special pudding. I'll just go and fetch it." And off she bustled to the kitchen.

Suddenly there was a loud shriek … and a clattering of pots … then a loud, rude burp!

"Help! HELP!" cried Mrs Williams.

Her nephews rushed to the kitchen and found her shaking all over, holding her best – empty –

serving dish, and pointing out of the window in disbelief. There, stomping off towards the woods, and trampling all over Mrs Williams' best geraniums as he went, was a large, wobbly, purple Monster … rubbing his tummy.

"It's the Jelly Monster!" squealed the two boys.

Word quickly spread round the village that a greedy, gobbling Jelly Monster was at large, spoiling picnics and gate-crashing parties.

People started going to parties in disguise so the Monster wouldn't know where they were going! Children tiptoed to friends' houses wearing huge raincoats, false moustaches and large-brimmed hats to cover their party clothes. But the Jelly Monster always seemed to know what was going on.

People tried having their parties in secret places – in the garden shed, or under the stairs. But the Jelly Monster still managed to sniff them out and gobble up all their jelly.

It wasn't long before everyone decided that something had to be done to stop the Jelly Monster. The vicar held a large meeting in the Church Hall to decide what to do.

"He spoilt my birthday," yelled Jenny Jones.

"He absolutely ruined my Tea Party," complained Mrs Hepplewhite.

"I spent hours making all those jellies for the old people's outing," said Mrs Fairweather, "and he scoffed the lot."

"He's a nuisance," they said.

"Get rid of him," they cried.

"No more Jelly Monster!"

The vicar calmed everyone down and said, "I have a suggestion. We should have a huge Jelly Eating Competition. The Jelly Monster is bound to turn up and eat up all the jelly. But there will be so much jelly that he'll be well and truly sick of it by the time he's finished and won't ever want to eat it again!!"

"HURRAY!" everyone shouted and began to make plans.

The Great Day arrived. People put out their tables and chairs on the Village Green. Kettles whistled as they boiled gallons of water to make the jelly. And everyone who had a fridge squashed in as many jellies as they could.

The band played and the Mayor declared the Jelly Eating Competition open.

The competitors sat round the tables, spoons at the ready, greedily watching the trays and trays of jelly being served.

But the Jelly Monster was nowhere to be seen.

The vicar stood holding his large pocket watch, carefully watching the second hand tick round to twelve.

"Ten seconds!" he announced. "Five seconds … three, two, one … Begin!"

The air rang with the clattering of spoons. And then a loud ROAR shook the ground. The Jelly Monster had found them!

"MMMmmm! Yummy jelly for me and my tummy." He gave a huge slurp, and before you could say, "wibble, wobble," he had gobbled all of the jelly on the first table. People ran to hide under tables and chairs, up in trees and behind bushes.

"MORE JELLY!" cried the Jelly Monster, banging the table impatiently. The jelly carriers scurried out with more jelly and the Monster ate it all up, slurping and burping and roaring, "MORE JELLY!"

Gradually, people came out from under the tables and down from the trees and gathered around the Jelly Monster, watching in amazement as he gulped down more and more jelly and grew huger and huger. Jelly was still coming thick and fast, but the Monster was beginning to slow

down. He was having to force down each spoonful.

"More jelly," he said in a feeble little voice.

At last all the jelly had been eaten and the monster sat back, holding his vast tummy. "More," he groaned.

"But all the jelly has gone, Mr Monster," said the Mayor politely.

"I want jelly," growled the Jelly Monster.

"Don't you think you should stop now. You have eaten rather a lot and you have won the competition. In fact," went on the Mayor, "you don't look very well ..."

"MORE!" thundered the

Jelly Monster.

A little girl walked out of the crowd towards the Jelly Monster. Everyone went quiet and watched, terrified that he would gobble her up...

"I have a little jelly you can have, Mr Monster," she said quietly. "I was saving it for my little brother who is poorly at home and couldn't come to the competition."

"Don't care," said the Jelly Monster. "Gimme, gimme!"

The little girl put the jelly in front of the Jelly Monster and crept back into the crowd. The Monster dug his spoon into the jelly, burping loudly.

The first mouthful went down very slowly. The second mouthful took ages. And the last mouthful only just squelched down! He tried to stand up.

"I'm the winner!" he growled and his tummy rumbled loudly. And the rumble grew louder and louder. His tummy quivered, his eyes bulged, his cheeks ballooned. The rumbling became so loud everyone covered their ears and closed their eyes. And then there was the most enormous explosion.

When everyone opened their eyes all they could see was a snowfall of wobbly bits of half-chewed jelly – and no Jelly Monster.

"Hurray! No more Jelly Monster!" Everyone shouted.

But secretly the villagers felt a bit sorry for the poor old Jelly Monster. What a horrible end! And it was a very long time before any of them felt like eating jelly again!

THE STORY OF
RORY MACAULAY

by Kate Petty

When people met Rory Macaulay,
who was quite small, with ordinary
fairish hair and bluish eyes, they

sometimes said to him, "Why Rory, you're as quiet as a mouse! With a name like yours I was expecting you to roar like a lion!" And then they laughed at their own joke and poor Rory felt very shy and wanted to disappear behind Mum or Dad or his big sister Alison.

But Rory wasn't shy with people he knew well. He liked talking to Grandpa and Granny and especially Uncle Hamish. They talked to him about interesting things and so he never even thought about being shy with them.

Best of all Rory liked talking about pirates. He knew almost everything there is to know about pirates. He knew that they wore eyepatches and earrings. He knew that they had missing teeth, missing eyes, and pegs for missing legs and hooks for missing hands. He knew the sails of pirate ships were black with a skull and crossbones on them. He knew their swords were called cutlasses and their rum was called grog. He knew all about walking the plank and digging for treasure.

Sometimes Grandpa and Uncle Hamish played wonderful pirate games with Rory. They turned the whole front room into the stormy sea and all the furniture into ships and islands. And together they sailed off into the afternoon in search of adventure, until it was time for ship's biscuits and grog in the kitchen with Mum and Aunty Mairie.

"My! I could hear you were having an uproarious time!" Aunty Mairie would say, laughing, and then Rory would laugh too, because he didn't mind Aunty Mairie making that sort of joke.

But when other people came to the house Rory felt terribly shy. He hated going out to tea, too, and parties were a nightmare. But worst of all, Rory was soon to start school, and he wasn't looking forward to meeting all those new people one bit.

One bad day, a little boy called Sam came to visit. Rory managed to peep over the top of the sofa at him only once the whole time he was there.

Afterwards Mum said, "Well Rory, I think the time has come to make you feel a bit braver about meeting people. Perhaps you should pretend that you aren't Rory Macaulay at all, but a big fierce bear. Or a lion."

Rory shook his head.

"How about a giant? Or a wizard?"

"I know," said Rory, "I'll pretend I'm a pirate, fearless and bold! I won't say 'Hello'. I'll say, 'Ahoy there, me hearties! Aaar, botter me coddersnipes, if it ain't young Sam!'"

So the next time Rory went out to tea he pretended to be a pirate. But it didn't help. Rory stood there, looking just like Rory, and saying "Aaaaar!" and "Waggle me wotterspotters", and Sam just laughed and went off to watch the television. When Mum and Alison came to fetch him, Rory was hiding behind the sofa.

Alison hugged him. "Tell you what, Rory," she said. "Let's make you a pirate costume, and then people will see that you're a bold and fearless pirate. I'll make you an eyepatch."

And she did. She crayoned a piece of cardboard completely black and cut it out and threaded elastic in it. Mum found a dressing-up fireman's jacket with shiny buttons that looked quite piratey. Dad made him a cardboard cutlass, Uncle Hamish found some piratey trousers in a car boot sale and Grandpa dug out one of his red spotty handkerchiefs to tie round Rory's head. Aunty Mairie produced a single brass earring and Cousin Bonnie made him a splendid hook – just like Captain Hook's hand – from a coat hanger.

There! Now, when people came to Rory's house, he just put on his pirate's costume. Everyone treated him like a pirate. Babies cried when they saw him. Dogs hid under tables. And so long as he was dressed like a pirate, Rory didn't feel shy.

"That's good," said Mum to Dad. "So far. But what are we going to do when he starts school? He can't wear grey shorts, a red tie and an eyepatch. And he'll never learn to write with a hook for a hand!"

"He's bound to grow out of it," said Dad. "I'm sure he'll be fine once he meets lots of new friends."

"But that's just the problem," said Mum. "How are we ever going to get him to meet these new friends without pretending to be a pirate?"

"Rory will be fine," chipped in Uncle Hamish. "Something will happen, just you see."

And it did.

One morning, Mum, Alison and Rory arrived home from buying some new clothes for school, just as the phone was ringing. Rory sat on the stairs and listened to Mum's half of the conversation. "A birthday party?... Thank you...Yes,

I'm sure Rory would love to come."

Rory scowled.

"A fancy-dress party! Yes, that's fine, we'll find something for Rory to wear... Thanks very much... Goodbye!"

Rory smiled. "I can go as a pirate, can't I, Mum? When is it? When can I go?"

"Saturday," said Mum. "That gives you three days to polish your cutlass!" Mrs Macaulay was delighted. Here at last was a party that Rory was looking forward to.

On Saturday Rory looked really splendid dressed up in his pirate costume. Alison had even blacked out some of his teeth and drawn some grizzly stubble on to his chin. Just as he was leaving for Sam's party, Uncle Hamish drew up in his van.

"Not so fast, ye blaggard! I've got something extra for your costume!" he said and handed Rory a plastic carrier bag with something in it.

"Look inside!"

Rory let go of his hook and his cutlass and looked in the bag. What could it be? He put in his hand and pulled out – a brightly-plumed toy parrot with bendy claws.

"Uncle Hamish, it's brilliant!" cried Rory and flung his arms around Uncle Hamish's knees.

Uncle Hamish perched the toy parrot on Rory's shoulder and off he went to the fancy-dress party feeling like the best-dressed pirate in the world. By the time he got to Sam's house he was really excited. Sam opened the door.

Goodness! Sam was dressed as a pirate too! "Ahoy there, Rory!" he said in a growly voice.

"Ahoy there, Sam!" Rory growled back, and together they marched into the room where everyone else was gathered. There was a witch and a ghost and a fairy. There was a nurse and a wizard and someone with a cardboard box on his head. Tweedledum and Tweedledee were there. So was Alice and the wizard's sister, who was dressed in a black plastic rubbish sack. And there were THREE MORE PIRATES! But none of them had such a practised swagger and snarl as Rory. And none of them had a parrot like Rory's.

"Ahoy there!" snarled Rory, feeling like the king of pirates.

"Ahoy there!" they all said back.

Rory wasn't a bit shy amongst all these strange new people.

Even when they played Blind Man's Buff, and danced the Hokey Cokey and ran a three-legged race, and got so hot that they had to take off most of their pirate gear, Rory

didn't mind. The parrot fell in the jelly and had to be washed, and Rory had to take off his hook to eat, but he was still enjoying himself.

When Mum came to collect him Rory introduced his new friends.

"Meet Pirate Harry and Pirate Jack, Pirate Amy and, of course, Pirate Sam," said Rory.

"Well, this is a nice surprise," said Mum. "Pleased to meet you, Pirate Harry, Pirate Jack, Pirate Amy and, of course, Pirate Sam."

And then, clutching their party bags and their balloons, it was time to say goodbye. Harry and Jack and Amy and Sam and their mums all said, "Goodbye Rory! See you next week!"

"Where will I see them again, Mum?" Rory asked on the way home.

"At school," said Mum. "Several pirates seem to be starting this term."

"I'm not sure I really need to be a pirate any more," said Rory. "But it will be nice to go to school with all my pirate friends. Think of all the games we'll be able to play."

Mrs Macaulay smiled down at her little pirate. She was going to miss him when he started school.

"But I'll still dress up as a pirate and play with Uncle Hamish when he comes to see us," said Rory, brandishing his cutlass.

"Oh, well that's all right then," laughed Mrs Macaulay, as Rory roared round the corner and home.

FRANKIE'S FRIEND
by Robin Kingsland

When Frankie's family moved to a
new town, Frankie had to say
goodbye to nearly all her old
friends. The only one who went

with her was Bad Archie.

No one except Frankie could see Bad Archie, but he went everywhere with her. He even sat next to her in the removals van.

When Frankie got to the new house she said, "I'll go out and make some new friends." But she didn't know how, so she asked Bad Archie.

"Easy," Bad Archie said. "Everyone will be your friend if they know your mum and dad are famous."

"But they're not famous," Frankie sighed.

"Pretend," said Bad Archie.

So Frankie pretended. She told

the first girl she met that her dad was a spaceman.

She told the first boy she met that her mum was Princess Di's Aunty.

She told the second boy she met that her dad was a racing driver.

But the first girl she'd met was listening and she said, "I thought your dad was a spaceman."

Frankie felt very stupid and ran home crying. She told her mum what had happened.

"Frankie," her mum said, "that sort of pretending isn't pretending. It's lying. And lying is a bad thing."

Bad Archie had another idea. "All the children will love you if you give them sweets!"

Frankie took all her sweets out to play, and started handing them out. But she only had a few chews. The same children kept coming back for second, third and even fourth chews. But the moment Frankie's last sweet disappeared, so did her 'friends'.

"I've got a brilliant idea this time," Bad Archie said next day. "Why don't you show off your cartwheels?"

Frankie was good at cartwheels. So she cartwheeled until she thought her arms would drop off. She did handstands until her face went red and her ears rang. But when she stopped she saw that the other children had already gone home.

"It's no good," Frankie told Bad Archie later. "I'll never make any friends."

But next morning Bad Archie had yet another plan. "This can't fail. If you want friends, start a gang. You can be the leader."

By lunchtime Frankie had a gang. "What shall we do?" Frankie asked them.

"You're the leader, you decide," the gang said.

Bad Archie whispered an idea in Frankie's ear.

"Right," said Frankie. "We'll knock on people's doors and run away. It will be fun."

By tea-time, no one in the gang
was talking to Frankie because
they'd all been sent to bed.

Frankie cried when her mum told
her off.

"Archie told me to do it," she
wailed.

"Well, that was very, very wrong
of him," Mum said. "And you can
tell him that from me."

But when Frankie went to tell
Bad Archie, she couldn't find him
anywhere. She looked in the shops.
She looked in the playground. A
girl called Kitty asked her what she
was looking for.

"I'm looking for my friend," said Frankie, and she told Kitty all about Bad Archie.

"He gets you into a lot of trouble, doesn't he?" Kitty said.

Frankie nodded.

"Why don't you come over here and meet my friends," said Kitty.

And so Frankie met Kitty's friends. They played all that day. And the next day. And the next day.

Frankie has lots of friends now. She hasn't seen Bad Archie for a long time, but I don't think she misses him that much!

THE RED JERSEY
by Janie Hampton

Sam was playing with his favourite
teddy when his mum came in.

"Come on," she said. "It's time
we sorted out your clothes."

"I don't want to sort out my clothes," said Sam. "That's a really boring job. Teddy wants to play with me. Why do you need me to help?"

"You've grown such a lot that some of your clothes are too small now. We need to see which ones still fit you and then we can take the old ones to the jumble sale this afternoon. It won't take long."

"She always says that," thought Sam. "It won't take long." And he went on playing with Teddy. Then he heard Mum throwing things around the bedroom. So he peeked round his bedroom door.

The drawers were all open. Mum

was pulling clothes out of the drawers on to the floor.

"That looks fun," thought Sam. "I didn't know Mum meant we could make a mess."

"Can I help?" said Sam.

"Of course. We'll put all your clothes into piles and decide what to keep."

So Sam pulled all the socks and the pants and the T-shirts and the trousers and the jerseys on to the floor.

"Let's start with the socks," said Mum. The socks were mixed up in a big pile.

"None of these are in pairs. Can you put them together – one brother and one sister?"

Sam held up a sock and looked for a pair – first a red one, then a blue one and then a striped one. Sam sang as he searched for the socks,

"Here's a red one, now where's its brother?

Here's a blue one, ah, there's the other.

Here's a striped one looking for a sister,

And where's the other little blister?"

There were lots of socks left over. "What's happened to their brothers and sisters?" asked Sam.

"The sock fairy must have taken them," Mum told him.

"What's a sock fairy?"

"Sock fairies only have one foot, so they need only one sock at a time. They are very forgetful, and they often lose socks, so then they hop into the house and take one of yours."

"Shall we leave the odd socks out for the sock fairy?" asked Sam.

"Or we can use them as dusters, or make sock-gloves, like this." Mum put her hand in the sock and made sock-faces at Sam.

Sam put his two favourite odd socks on Teddy.

"Now we must do the other clothes," said Mum. "Stand still while I see if this still fits."

Sam stood with his back to Mum as she held the clothes against him. She put the good clothes back into the drawers. The ones with holes she put in a pile for rags to clean the house. The good clothes that were too small she put in a pile to go to the jumble sale.

Mum held a red jersey with an engine knitted into it against Sam's back. It was too small.

"I'm bored with this," said Sam. "I want to go and play. T-shirts and things don't have brothers and sisters like socks do."

"Go on then," said Mum. "I've nearly finished."

A little later Mum and Sam set

out for the jumble sale. Mum carried a bag of old clothes. Sam carried his teddy.

"Do you have to bring Teddy?" asked Mum.

"Yes, he wants to come," said Sam. "He needs the fresh air."

The jumble sale was at the playgroup. There were piles of clothes on a long table and a pile of toys on the floor.

Sam hung his coat up on his peg.

"Put Teddy inside your coat pocket so you won't forget him," said Mum.

While Mum helped to sell the clothes, Sam looked at the toys.

Sam didn't think much of them.
The books had no covers. The
jigsaw puzzle had lost half its bits.
The doll had no arms.

Lots of people came in and
rummaged through the clothes.
They threw some over their
shoulders.

"How much is this?"

"What do you want for this one?"
they shouted.

A red jersey landed beside Sam.
He looked closer and picked it up.

"This is a nice jersey," he
thought. "It's just like my favourite
jersey at home. I'll ask Mum to buy
it."

Mum was busy selling a dress to a

nice old lady.

"Yes it is a lovely colour isn't it, Mrs Green?" said Mum.

"I like purple," said Mrs Green. "It would just do for my summer holiday. How much is it then?"

"Fifty pence to you, Mrs Green," said Mum.

"Mum, Mum," said Sam, tugging at Mum's sleeve. "I want to buy this jersey."

"You don't want to buy that, Sammy dear," said Mum.

"But I do," said Sam. "It's the pair of the one at home, like a pair of socks. I've found its brother.

"It doesn't fit you, it's too small," said Mum.

"How do you know? I haven't tried it on."

"Yes you have. It's your old jersey, you've grown out of it. That's why I brought it here to sell to someone else."

"But it's my favourite jersey! You never asked me!" cried Sam.

"I tried to ask you, but you went away when I was sorting the jerseys," explained Mum.

This wasn't the brother of Sam's favourite engine jersey after all. It was his very own, one-and-only best jersey!

Sam tried to pull it on, but it got stuck round his neck.

"You see. What did I tell you?"

said Mum. "It's too small"

"I don't care if it's too small," said Sam "I still want it."

Mrs Green smiled at Sam. "Can I buy it?" she said. "I know someone who might just fit it."

"No, it's mine," said Sam.

Sam looked glum as Mrs Green gave Mum twenty pence for the jersey.

Sam was very cross. He hid under the table of clothes for the rest of the afternoon.

"Come on, Sam," said Mum later. "Time to go home."

"I don't want to go home. Ever," said Sam.

"Well you can't stay here," said

Mum. "Everybody else has gone and we're locking up now. Go and get your coat."

Sam went to his peg and took down his coat. Teddy was still inside the pocket.

"Look!" cried Sam suddenly. "Teddy's wearing my red engine jersey!"

Mrs Green had bought the jersey for Sam's teddy! It didn't fit Sam anymore, but it had found a good home somewhere else. And what with the odd socks and the red engine jersey, Sam thought that Teddy looked the smartest teddy bear in the world.